W9-AOP-820

Miranda's Beach Day

HOLLY KELLER

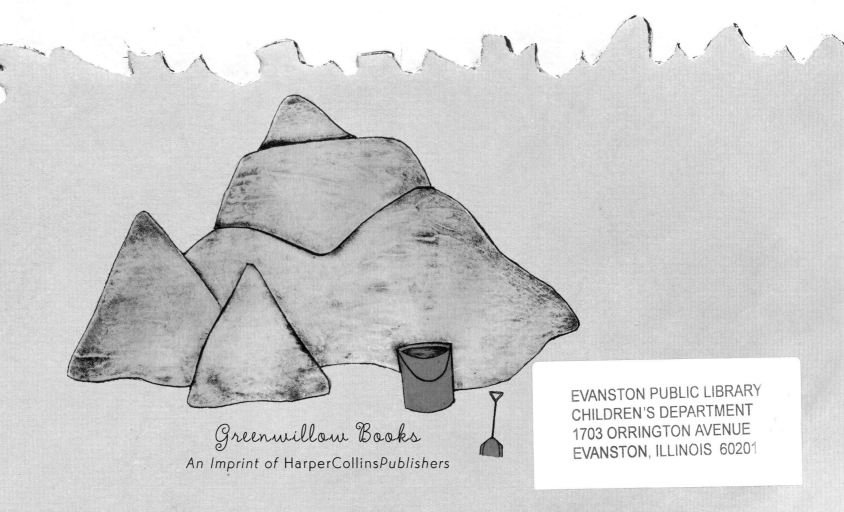

Greenwillow Books
An Imprint of HarperCollinsPublishers

Miranda's Beach Day

Copyright © 2009 by Holly Keller

All rights reserved. Manufactured in China.

www.harpercollinschildrens.com

The text type is 22-point Martin Gothic Medium.

Library of Congress Cataloging-in-Publication Data

Keller, Holly.

Miranda's beach day / by Holly Keller.

p. cm.

"Greenwillow Books."

Summary: Miranda and Mama spend a fun day at the beach building castles and catching sand crabs
and Miranda learns that just like the sand and the sea, she and her mother will always be together.

ISBN 978-0-06-158298-1 (trade bdg.) — ISBN 978-0-06-158300-1 (lib. bdg.)

[1. Beaches—Fiction. 2. Mother and child—Fiction.] I. Title.

PZ7.K28132Mi 2009   [E]—dc22   2008012645

First Edition 10 9 8 7 6 5 4 3 2 1

 Greenwillow Books

For Zoë

One hot summer day,

Mama took Miranda to the beach.

"It's hot enough to cook an egg on the sand," Mama said.

"Really?" asked Miranda.

"No," said Mama, "but it feels like it."

Mama carried the towels.

Miranda carried her new pail and shovel.

The sand was so hot that it shimmered.

Some seagulls in the sky were squawking.

"Are they laughing or crying?" asked Miranda.

"I think they're hungry," said Mama.

The breeze blew Miranda's hair.

Salty sand stuck to her face.

"I like the beach," she said.

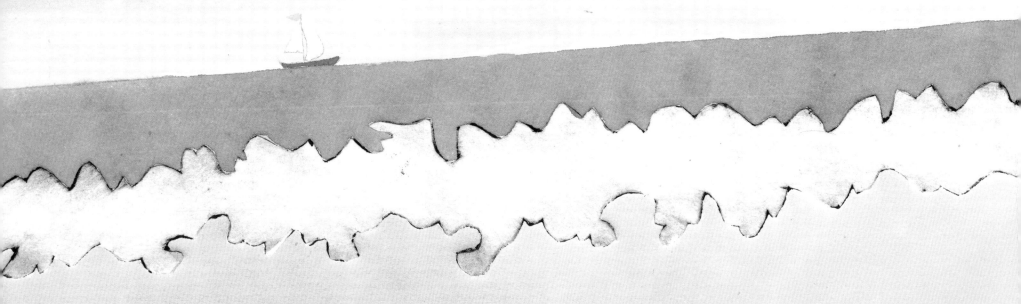

In the water, Miranda's toes were cold.

She pushed them into the wet sand.

When a wave came, Miranda plopped onto her bottom
and let the water swirl around her.

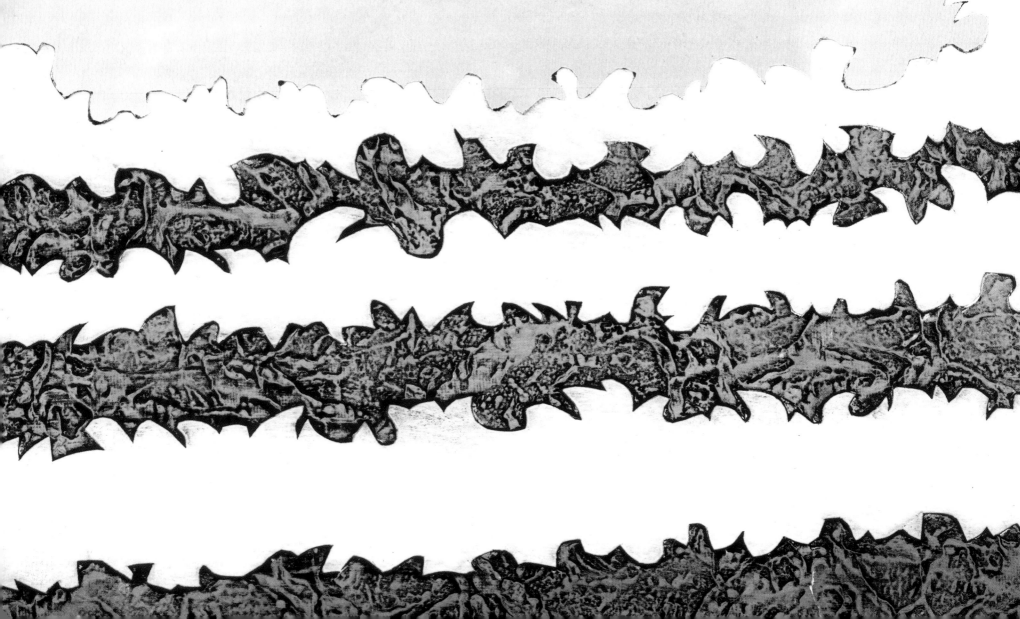

"Swish, swish," said Miranda,
and she wiggled her feet.
"I'm a mermaid."

A small crab walking sideways stopped near Mama's foot.

He was carrying a shell.

"The shell is his house," Mama said.

"It's not a very big one," said Miranda.

"I'll build him a castle."

Miranda scooped up the crab and put him into her pail.

She started to dig.

A boy named Raymond came over to watch.

"You can help, if you want to," said Miranda.

Raymond used a plastic cone to make towers.

His little sister came over to help, too.

They dug and piled and smoothed the sand.

They worked all afternoon.

"It's the best castle ever,"

said Miranda when it was finished.

Miranda dug a deep hole for the door

and put the crab inside.

"There," she said.

"Now you have a new house."

But the crab scurried right out
and raced back to the water.
He was still carrying his old house.
"I'll catch him," shouted Miranda.
"You had better hurry," said Mama.
"The tide is coming in."

A big wave washed up on the beach.

It made a roaring sound.

The castle became an island.

Another wave spread over the sand

and the castle was gone.

"It was a beautiful castle," said Mama.

"We'll come again another day

and you can make a new one."

"Will the crab be here again, too?" Miranda asked.

"Yes," said Mama, "but the crab

will always belong to the sea."

"The way the castle belongs to the sand?"

asked Miranda.

"Yes," Mama said.

"And the way you belong to me."

A Note from Holly Keller

Parts of the illustrations for *Miranda's Beach Day* were painted with watercolors, and other parts were created with printed collages. A collage can be made of cut cardboard, paper, string, and many other materials, which are pasted together to form an image (Photo 1). To make these illustrations, I coated my collages with acrylic gesso so they could be inked and printed (Photo 2). I used an oil-based etching ink, and the printing was done on a large-bed etching press (Photo 3). The paper I used is Rives BFK. A printed collage is called a collagraph, and it reproduces on paper all of the interesting textures of the original collage (Photo 4). My last step was to color the collagraphs with watercolors.

1

2

3

4